EVERYDAY SAINTS

STORIES OF QUIET COURAGE

C.E. ALBANESE

GNAW BONE PUBLISHING, LLC

CONTENTS

A NOTE ON SAINTHOOD

Sainthood is not reserved for the distant past or for the extraordinarily devout. Nor is this title limited to those who perform miracles or bear the wounds of martyrdom. The saints among us are often hidden in plain sight. They're the teacher who sees potential in a troubled student, the neighbor who shares what little she has with others, the brother who prays through the wall when words fail, or the elderly volunteer.

In Catholic tradition, we speak of the "communion of saints"—that great fellowship of souls who have lived lives of heroic virtue. But heroism, we discover, often looks quite ordinary. It appears in the daily choice to serve rather than be served, to love when love seems foolish, to hope when hope feels impossible.

Though fictional in form, these stories spring from lived experiences and explore what St. Thérèse of Lisieux called "the little way," where we can find God not in grand gestures but in simple faithfulness. These are saints who will never be canonized, whose names will never grace cathedral windows, yet whose quiet holiness transforms the world one small act at a time.

Perhaps this is the most profound truth about sainthood: it is not about perfection, but about surrender. It is not about being extraordinary, but about allowing the extraordinary love of God to work through our very ordinary lives.

In the end, every saint began as someone who simply said yes to love, and kept saying yes, one moment at a time, until love became their native language and service their natural response to the grace they had received.

The saints are all around us. They teach our children, serve our meals, hold our hands in prayer. They remind us that holiness is not a destination but a way of traveling, and that the path is open to anyone willing to walk it with an open heart. You. Me. Everyone is called to become a saint. The question is, will you answer the call?

THE DIVORCE PAPERS

*K*im spread the divorce papers across the kitchen table for the third time this month, her pen hovering over the signature line. The lawyer's words echoed: *Given his addiction, reconciliation is unlikely. You need to protect yourself.*

Three months of unsigned documents. Three months of silence from David except for the automated texts from rehab: *Patient checked out against medical advice. Patient readmitted. Patient checked out.*

A scream built in her chest. The burn within grew. Seconds passed. She gripped her knees, wishing... for what? The courage to sign, or the strength to tear them up entirely.

Lips tight, she exhaled through her nose, followed by five quick breaths. She turned toward the window.

Tired eyes caught the reflection. She didn't see herself.

Mom?

The image shifted. Sharper now.

Grandma Rita?

Not the frail woman she'd buried. The stoic one, who knew how to change a tire and how to swing a hammer... and how to pray.

The memory landed hard. Grandma's weathered hands folded in

prayer every night, whispering words passed down like a family recipe.

After Grandpa came back from Vietnam, hollow-eyed and unreachable, Grandma lit a candle and prayed to her namesake saint —*Rita of Cascia, patron of impossible marriages.*

"Things got worse before they got better," Grandma used to say, in her tough New York accent. "But prayer isn't about getting what you want. It's about staying faithful to what you love."

Kim found a votive in the junk drawer, lit it with trembling hands. The flame wavered, then steadied. She closed her eyes and whispered the words Grandma taught her:

Holy Rita, you who endured so much pain in your marriage, intercede for us who struggle to hold love together when it's falling apart. Help us find the strength to stay faithful, even when faith feels impossible.

The candle burned down to nothing. Kim folded the papers and slipped them and the pen back in the drawer. She'd try again tomorrow.

Tomorrow came. And with it, David.

Thirty days sober, the longest streak in two years. His eyes were clear. Not just clean. Present.

"I know you have papers to sign," he said, voice rough with unused words. "I know I have no right to ask. But I'm here. I'm really here this time."

Kim looked at him—this man she'd married, lost, grieved while he was still breathing. The divorce papers waited in the drawer, unsigned. Between them hung everything broken. Everything that might still be possible.

She stepped back from the doorway and let him in.

The candle holder sat on the table, waxy and empty. But somewhere in the house, Grandma Rita's prayer lingered like smoke. Like hope. Like the kind of faith that outlasts reason.

ENTIENDO

am slumped in the chair, staring at the scuffed linoleum. The guidance counselor's words barely registered:
"They want to kick you out."

He glanced up, caught that look in the counselor's eyes. The same one everyone had after his father died.

"But your mom and I got them to agree to let you sit in Mr. Evans' classroom," the counselor added.

"Great." Sam slouched further. "You're shipping me off to the land of misfits and freaks."

"I think you'll find Mr. Evans is exactly what you need."

"Yeah?" Sam pushed himself up to his feet, muscles taut. "What's that?"

"A teacher who gets you."

Sam snorted. "No one gets me." He whipped around, yanked the door open. "No one."

Walking down the hallway, Sam expected chaos inside Mr. Evans' classroom. Instead, the so-called "land of outcasts" was calm.

Ten students sat quietly reading. Soft classical music hummed through a pair of speakers. Sam recognized the sad, haunting melody. "Moonlight Sonata." *Dad's favorite.*

At the front of the classroom stood Mr. Evans—bald, with a snow-white goatee and glasses perched on his nose. Santa Claus without the belly. Behind him, a picture of some guy labeled as St. John Bosco hung on the wall, with the inscription: *'It is not enough to love young people; they must know they are loved.'*

Love. Sam's jaw tightened. *Right.*

He plopped down in an empty seat in the back.

Mr. Evans slid a copy of *The Odyssey* onto Sam's desk. "You'll need to catch up, but if you're anything like your older sister, it shouldn't be a problem."

My older sister? He shoved the book off his desk.

Mr. Evans picked it up, placing it back gently.

Sam tapped his fingers on the cover, waiting for a lecture that never came.

Day two. Sam noticed things were different in this classroom. Kids actually participated. Asked questions. Were respectful and polite.

When Mr. Evans called on him, Sam replied in Spanish, "No hablo Inglés."

Mr. Evans nodded. "Entiendo. Cuando estés listo." *I understand. When you're ready.*

Sam blinked.

Mr. Evans gestured to the wall, switching back to English. "Don Bosco believed every kid just needed someone to see the good in them. I see you, Sam. I see the good."

Me? Good? Sam's eyes flicked to the portrait, then away.

Day three was the anniversary. One year since that drunk driver killed his dad. Mom worked double shifts now, barely scraping together rent and his sister's college tuition. Perfect Sarah, star athlete, valedictorian. Nobody cared about the angry kid left behind.

After class, Marcus, another "problem" kid, brushed past Sam, clipping his shoulder. Fist balled, arm cocked, Sam swung—and missed. Marcus didn't. Two blows. One to the side of Sam's head, the other smashing into his gut.

Mr. Evans broke it up, pulling Sam back inside the classroom.

"I know you're angry at the world," Mr. Evans said quietly. "I know how it feels to lose someone."

"How could you possibly know?" Sam's voice cracked.

"Lost my brother when I was sixteen. Spent two years picking fights, getting kicked out of places." He paused. "Anger's easier than grief."

"Yeah." Sam's eyes found his shoes. "It is."

Day four. Sam expected to be called down to the principal's office. Thought he'd get a message from his counselor. Nothing. Only Mr. Evans announcing, "Read whatever you want today. No limits."

Sam stared at his empty desk. Around him, other kids pulled out books, notebooks, even comics. The room settled into peaceful silence.

Slowly, Sam reached into his backpack and pulled out *The Odyssey*. He flipped to page one and began reading about a hero trying to find his way home.

For the first time in months, the words on a page held his attention. Odysseus was angry too. Had lost everything. But kept going.

Maybe there was something to this after all. Something he couldn't quite name, but definitely felt. *Don't get soft*, he warned himself.

Without thinking, his eyes found the portrait of St. John Bosco. Then Mr. Evans, who offered a slight nod and a reassuring smile. Sam almost smiled back. Almost. But he did return the nod.

CRISIS LINE

*R*honda adjusted her headset and stared at the phone, willing it not to ring. Her first solo shift. After a week of intensive training and two days of shadowing experienced volunteers, she thought she was ready. Public service was a college requirement, and this seemed perfect, though she wished it paid. Still, helping someone in need felt like compensation enough. Besides, she loved talking on the phone, had always been the one her friends called with their problems. Mom said she'd inherited the gift from her. But Rhonda knew better. She was all Dad—level-headed, compassionate, with answers that somehow always helped.

How hard could it be?

The phone rang.

Her stomach dropped. She took a breath and answered. "Crisis helpline, this is Rhonda."

Silence. Then, barely audible: "I... I don't know why I called."

A young voice. Female. Scared.

"That's okay," Rhonda said, falling back on her training. "Sometimes it helps just to talk. I'm here to listen."

More silence. Rhonda waited, fighting the urge to fill the space with words. Something else she remembered from the training.

"I'm in trouble," the voice finally said. "Bad trouble. And I don't... I can't..." The words dissolved into quiet sobs.

Rhonda's confident façade cracked. This wasn't like consoling her roommate after a breakup. Or her younger sisters when Mom or Dad scolded them. This was real pain. Raw. Desperate. She recalled something from orientation: *You can't fix someone's life in one phone call. But you can help them take the next step. Sometimes that's enough to save them.*

She pulled her chair closer to the desk. "Are you safe right now?" she asked gently.

A pause. Then: "I guess."

"Can you tell me your name?"

A longer pause. "It's a stupid name. Caused me nothing but grief my whole life. My mom heard it somewhere and thought it sounded pretty."

"I bet it's not stupid at all."

A huff. "Dymphna. See? Told you. Stupid."

Rhonda's breath caught. Of all the names... "Actually, I know that name. It's beautiful—"

"You don't have to lie."

"I'm not. You're named after a beautiful Irish saint."

"A saint? You're kidding."

"No, really. Saint Dymphna. There's even a shrine to her in my hometown—Massillon, Ohio. Inside St. Mary's Church."

"What's her story? It's gotta be better than mine."

For the first time, Rhonda heard something besides despair in the girl's voice. Pain, yes—but also curiosity. She closed her eyes, remembering the stained-glass windows from childhood Masses.

"She was an Irish princess who had to run away from home. After her mother died, her father wanted... a relationship that wasn't right. So she fled, looking for somewhere safe."

"She ran away too, huh?" Dymphna whispered.

"Yeah. It was scary—being in a foreign place with nothing. But she found people who helped her. She spent the rest of her life creating safe places for others who were hurting."

Silence stretched, but this time it felt different.

7

"I've been on the streets for over a month," Dymphna said finally. Her voice was steadier now. "Dad's in prison—life sentence. Mom's... well, she's probably passed out at some bar right now. Doesn't matter what time it is." The words tumbled out now, as if a dam had burst. "She'd bring random guys home. Sometimes they'd find their way to my bedroom..." Dymphna took a shuddered breath. "I thought the streets would be safer. But they're not. Nothing's been good for me. And last night..." Her voice trailed off.

Rhonda's hands trembled. This girl was maybe sixteen. Alone. Hopeless. "What happened, Dymphna?"

"I was... someone... they hurt me. Worse than anything any of my mom's boyfriends ever did. I can't even..." Her voice broke. "I'm ready to end it all. The pain, the suffering. There's no future for me."

Rhonda gripped the phone, feeling the weight of this moment. Every instinct screamed that she wasn't qualified for this. But Dymphna was still on the line. Still talking. Still hoping.

"The pain is real," Rhonda said quietly. "But so is hope. St. Dymphna thought there was no way out either. But she found sanctuary. She found healing. And she used her pain to help others."

"You really think there's hope for someone like me?"

"I know there is. There are people who want to help—shelters, counselors, people who understand. You don't have to do this alone. You're not alone."

Dymphna was crying again, but softer now. "There's a shelter downtown. I walked past it yesterday but was too scared to go in."

"Would you be willing to try? Just to see?"

"Maybe. If... if you think they'd really help."

"I do. And Dymphna? Your name isn't stupid. It means you're named after someone brave enough to seek safety when she needed it."

A soft snort. "I'm the furthest from brave."

"You called this number, didn't you? That *is* brave. That's the first step."

A beat of silence.

"Can I... can I call you tomorrow? Maybe... just to talk."

Rhonda glanced at the schedule board. Tomorrow was Saturday. Her day off. She had plans to see a movie with her parents and siblings. But she heard herself say, "Definitely. I'll be here for you tomorrow. And the next day. And the day after that."

A pause. Then, softly: "Okay. Tomorrow, then."

After they hung up, Rhonda sat in the quiet room, understanding for the first time what her father's compassion really meant. It wasn't about having easy answers. It was about showing up, even when— especially when—you felt inadequate.

She walked to the supervisor's office and knocked.

"I'd like to pick up some extra shifts."

WARD SEVEN

*J*eanne tugged her wool coat tighter as she stepped out of the grocery store. Behind her, the automatic doors sealed shut with a soft whoosh. Christmas morning, and the world felt hushed under a gray sky that promised snow. Her arthritic fingers fumbled with her purse clasp. Inside, were last week's volunteer hospital badge and a small bag of saltines.

The walk home took longer these days. Every step sent sharp reminders up her legs, and her ankles had swollen again despite the compression stockings. But she didn't complain. Instead, she offered up the ache, the cold wind that bit at her cheeks, the fatigue that seemed to live in her bones now.

For the souls in purgatory, she whispered, same as every morning. *Especially for my Robert.*

At her small apartment, she fed the three cats who'd claimed her fire escape, then gathered the books from the shelf by the window into her canvas bag. Hardy Boys and Nancy Drew mysteries. The Harry Potter fantasies. *The Secret Garden.* The faded covers were soft from handling, from when her own children were small. Before time measured itself in decades instead of years.

The mile-long walk to Children's Hospital stretched before her, but she set out with purpose. *Do little things with great love*, she reminded herself, words from the young French saint she'd grown to cherish as she stepped from the sidewalk and shuffled across the street. St. Thérèse had called it "the little way." Small acts, done with enormous love, mattered as much to God as grand gestures. Jeanne's daily walks, her saltines for the pigeons, her volunteer hours—none of it would make headlines, but perhaps that was exactly the point.

In Meridian Park, she scattered saltines for the pigeons that waited by the old fountain, their gray heads bobbing in what looked like gratitude.

The hospital rose ahead, seven stories of windows that held more hope and heartbreak than she cared to contemplate. But today, like every Tuesday and Thursday for the past eight years, she entered through the sliding glass doors with nothing but hope and a smile.

"Morning, Ms. Jeanne." The security guard handed her a new volunteer badge without looking up. "Merry Christmas."

"Merry Christmas, Bobby. Your granddaughter feeling better?"

"Much better, thanks for asking. Seeing her after my shift."

"That's good to hear, Bobby. Please give her my love."

On the fifth floor, Nurse Patricia looked up from her station with relief. "Ward Seven's been asking for you. New patient in Room 329. Ten years old. Just diagnosed last week."

Jeanne nodded, her chest tightening in the familiar way. She'd learned not to ask for details. She'd get the story soon enough.

Room 329 was located at the end of the hallway, the soft beeping of monitors breaking the silence within. A small figure sat propped in the hospital bed, staring out the window at nothing. Thin brown hair, pale skin that spoke of too many hours indoors, dark eyes that looked too old for ten.

"Hi there," Jeanne said softly, settling into the chair beside the bed. "I'm Jeanne. I come by sometimes to read stories. Would you like that?"

The child turned slowly. "Are you a nurse?"

"No, honey. Just a volunteer. What's your name?"

"Casey." A pause. "I have cancer."

Jeanne set down her bag of books and met those old eyes with her own.

"I know, sweetheart. I'm sorry."

"Everyone's sorry." Casey's voice carried a bitterness that made Jeanne's heart clench. "The doctors are sorry. The nurses are sorry. Mom cried and said she was sorry. Dad hasn't even come yet. But he'll say he's sorry too."

"Sometimes sorry is all people know how to say."

Casey stared at the cross on her chain, not quite meeting Jeanne's eyes. "Are you going to tell me everything happens for a reason?"

"No."

"Are you going to say God has a plan?"

Jeanne was quiet, feeling the weight of the question and the challenge behind it. Through the window, snow had begun to fall in lazy flakes.

"Can I tell you something, Casey?"

The question was met with a shrug.

Jeanne scooted to the edge of the chair. "I have cancer too."

Casey's eyes sharpened. "You do?"

"Stage four. Breast cancer." The words came easier than she'd expected. "The doctors say I have maybe six months. Maybe more if I'm lucky."

"Then why are you here?" Casey's voice cracked slightly. "Why aren't you at home?"

Jeanne smiled, and for the first time, she saw something flicker in Casey's expression. Curiosity instead of anger.

"Because there's a little girl named Casey who needs someone to read her a story. And because sitting at home feeling sorry for myself doesn't make the cancer go away. But maybe—" She reached for the Dr. Seuss book. "Maybe reading *Green Eggs and Ham* for the hundredth time makes today just a little better than yesterday."

"That's a baby book."

"You're right. How about Nancy Drew? She's an amateur detective solving professional mysteries. My daughter loved these stories when she was your age."

Casey considered this. "I don't like mysteries. People always figure out the answer."

"What do you like?"

"Nothing anymore." The words came out flat, final.

Jeanne nodded. "I felt like that too." *Right after my husband's heart attack. And again when my son was killed in Afghanistan. And definitely last month when Dr. Peterson told me about the cancer.* But she kept those deeper losses to herself.

"How do you stop feeling like that?" Casey asked.

"I'm not sure you do. Not completely." Jeanne reached into her purse and pulled out a small wrapped candy bar—the same kind she had left at the grocery-store register that morning for the cashier with the kind eyes. "But maybe you find little things that still matter. Like making sure the pigeons in the park don't go hungry. Or reading to kids who are stuck in hospital beds on Christmas morning."

Casey took the candy bar, turning it over in small hands. She gestured to the cross. "Do you really believe in God?"

"With all of my heart."

"Even though He gave you cancer?"

"Even though."

"That's kinda dumb."

Jeanne laughed, a real laugh that surprised them both. "You'd think it was, right? But you know what? Sometimes I do get mad at God. But then I think about all the good things too. Like the fact that I got to raise three wonderful children. And that I lived long enough to volunteer here. And that I got to meet a very smart little girl named Casey who asks the hard questions."

"I'm not smart. Smart kids don't get cancer."

"Oh, honey." Jeanne reached over and touched Casey's hand, just barely. Just enough. "Cancer doesn't care. Not how smart you are, or how kind. Not if you're ten or seventy. It just is. Like rain. Like snow." She nodded toward the window. "Like Christmas morning."

They sat in comfortable silence, watching the snow fall. Finally, Casey spoke.

"My mom and dad are coming today. But not together. They can't be in the same room anymore."

"That must be hard."

"Everything's hard now." Casey unwrapped the candy bar and broke off a piece. "Will you stay? When they come?"

"If you want me to."

"I want you to." Casey handed Jeanne half of the candy bar. "And maybe you could read something. Not that mystery story. Something else."

Jeanne looked through her books and pulled out an old, worn copy. "How about *The Secret Garden*? It's about a little girl who helps things grow, even when everything seems hopeless."

Casey settled back against the pillows. "Okay. But if it gets too sad, I'm going to tell you to stop."

"Deal."

As Jeanne opened to the first page, she heard footsteps in the hallway. Probably Casey's mother arriving. Soon there would be tears and difficult conversations and the terrible dance of divorced parents trying to navigate their child's illness. But for now, there was just a story about gardens and hope, shared between two people who understood that faith wasn't always about answers. Sometimes, it was simply about showing up. About loving.

About *the little way*.

"When Mary Lennox was sent to Misselthwaite Manor to live with her uncle," Jeanne began, "everybody said she was the most disagreeable-looking child ever seen..."

Outside, the snow continued to fall, covering the world in something clean and new.

ROUTE CHANGE

Frank rubbed the St. Christopher medal with his thumb, same as every morning. The silver had worn smooth under countless touches, but the image remained clear—the saint carrying a child across rushing water.

"Morning, Frank." Supervisor Martinez climbed the steps, clipboard in hand. Never a good sign.

"Morning." Frank clipped the medal to the visor and started his pre-trip inspection.

"Got a problem. Three drivers called in sick, probably that stomach bug going around. Need you to cover Route 29."

Frank's hands stilled on the steering wheel. "That's the Eastside run."

"You know it, right? You worked it when you started."

Twenty-five years ago. When he was young and stupid and thought he could save the world one bus route at a time. Before he learned better. Before he requested the transfer to the suburbs where the worst thing that happened was an elderly passenger forgetting their stop.

"That was a long time ago, Martinez. Things have changed."

"Tell me about it. But you're the only driver this shift who knows those streets."

Frank had heard the stories from the guys who still worked the urban routes. Broken windows. Graffiti that cost more to clean than his monthly salary. Tommy Rodriquez came back last month with a black eye and three stitches. Said some kid sucker-punched him over a fare dispute.

"You offering hazard pay?"

Martinez snorted. "Look, Frank, it's one day. Maybe two."

Frank touched the medal again.

"I'm six months from retirement, Martinez. Six months."

"Which is why I need someone reliable. Someone who won't panic." Martinez stepped down from the bus. "Route starts at Crenshaw and Fifth. First pickup's at seven-thirty."

Frank stared at his reflection in the windshield. Behind the glass, an old man looked back—gray stubble, tired eyes, hands that shook slightly sometimes, though he tried not to think about why.

The medal caught the morning sun.

Twenty-five years ago, he'd carried hope along with passengers. Now he just wanted to make it to retirement without incident.

He started the engine and pulled out of the depot, heading east toward a part of the city he'd spent decades trying to forget.

The first stop was a corner market with bars on the windows. Three teenagers waited at the bus shelter, hoodies pulled up despite the warm weather. They climbed aboard without making eye contact, dropped exact change in the farebox, and took seats in the back.

Frank watched them in the mirror, taking in everything. One had fresh scratches on his knuckles. Another kept checking his phone, leg bouncing with nervous energy.

"Next stop, Crenshaw and Ninth," Frank announced.

No one responded.

Two more stops, six more passengers. An elderly woman with a walker who needed help getting seated. A young mother with twin toddlers who apologized three times for the crying. A man in paint-splattered jeans and work boots who smelled like coffee and cigarettes.

Normal people. Quiet people.

Frank started to relax. That was his first mistake.

"Give it back!"

In the mirror, Frank saw one of the teenagers—the one with scratched knuckles—standing over the elderly woman. Her purse was on the floor, contents scattered. The woman pressed herself against the window, walker clutched to her chest like a shield.

Frank's foot hovered over the brake. Protocol was clear: don't intervene directly. Call dispatch. Wait for police.

But the kid was reaching for the woman's walker now, probably trying to shake loose whatever money she had hidden there.

The medal swayed as the bus hit a pothole.

An image of St. Christopher carrying strangers across dangerous waters filled his mind. No questions asked. No guarantee of safety. Just the simple act of getting people where they needed to go.

Frank pulled the bus to the curb and stood up.

"Hey."

The teenager looked up, surprised. In that moment, Frank saw past the hoodie and the attitude to the scared kid underneath. Maybe sixteen. Maybe younger.

"Leave her alone, son."

"Son?" The kid glanced back at his buddies. "Mind your own business, old man."

Frank stepped into the aisle.

"This is my bus. These are my passengers. That makes it my business."

The other passengers had gone silent. Even the toddlers stopped crying.

Frank took another step forward. "You can get off now, or I can call the police. Your choice."

For a moment, nobody moved. Then the kid bent down, scooped the woman's belongings back into her purse, and handed it to her.

"Sorry," he mumbled.

He walked to the front of the bus, stopped at the door, then looked back at Frank.

"My grandma rides this route sometimes. Bus 47. She's about her age." He nodded toward the elderly woman. "I hope someone looks out for her too."

The door hissed open and he was gone.

Frank helped the woman check her purse. Nothing was missing. She patted his hand with fingers like tissue paper.

"Thank you, dear. You're a good man."

Frank returned to his seat, adjusted the medal on the visor. The circle of light had moved, but it was still there.

Six months until retirement. Maybe that was enough time to remember why he'd wanted to drive a bus in the first place.

He pulled back into traffic, heading toward the next stop.

FAITHFUL MESSENGER

$\mathcal{J}$im adjusted the rearview mirror as his trainer, Tory, climbed out of the mail truck for the last time.

"You've got the longest, prettiest route in the county," she said. "But also the safest. People out here respect what we do."

She reached up to the visor and retrieved a small prayer card tucked there. "They keep their dogs leashed too." She winked. "At least the unfriendly ones."

Jim had noticed the card all week but hadn't asked about it. Something about Tory's reverent touch made him curious now.

"St. Gabriel," she said, catching his glance. "Patron saint of messengers. Carried that card for fifteen years." She paused. "You Catholic?"

"Was. Long time ago." Jim's throat tightened. "Been feeling... called back lately."

Tory smiled. "He has a way of doing that." She patted the truck's dashboard. "Take care of this old girl. And take care of yourself. Call me if you get stuck tomorrow." She winked again. "Or lost."

The next morning, Jim found his own St. Gabriel prayer card tucked in the visor. Different from Tory's, but the same gentle-faced archangel. He read the simple, familiar words. Twice. Then, slipped the card back, leaving just the corner visible.

A twist of the key. The ignition caught and the truck came to life.

This wasn't what he'd expected to be doing at fifty-nine. Not at all. By now, he'd imagined himself a successful novelist, writing crime, mystery, thrillers where flawed heroes always saved the day. Instead, he was delivering mail in rural Washington state, hoping the quiet miles might finally give him stories to tell.

The hours zipped past. Days turned into weeks, yet the postal muse never appeared. No plot twists, no characters, no inspiration. Just the steady rhythm of mailboxes and the unexpected satisfaction of connecting people to their world.

Not a bad way to make a living, he thought. Honest, sure. Just not what he really wanted to do. Or believed was his life calling.

Until he pulled up to Mrs. Wexley's mailbox.

And there was no cookie.

Eleanor Wexley, a widow in her eighties, had become his favorite stop. She'd appear on her porch whenever she heard his truck, waving with genuine joy as if his arrival was the highlight of her day. Her homemade snickerdoodles, left in a small basket by the mailbox, had become Jim's afternoon treat. And maybe the reason he'd put on an extra couple pounds.

Today—September 29th, he noted—there was no Mrs. Wexley. No cookie. And yesterday's mail still sat untouched. Same for the old Buick parked in the carport.

In this part of the county, neighbors lived miles apart. Jim had no idea if Mrs. Wexley had family nearby, or family at all.

Something felt off. *No, not off.*

Wrong.

If Jim was working on his novel, he'd write that his protagonist had a gut feeling. The twisty, bad kind.

He parked and approached the front door. Three sharp knocks echoed across the porch. Nothing. Walking around back, he knocked again. The seconds dragged. His fingertips tingled. That gut feeling intensified. He leaned forward, putting his ear to the door.

A faint cry drifted from inside. "Help... please..."

Jim's heart hammered. *She's alive. Thank God, she's alive.* "Mrs.

Wexley?" Jim tried the door handle. Locked. "I'm getting help." He dialed 911.

"Sheriff's deputy will be there in twenty minutes," the dispatcher informed him.

Mrs. Wexley's voice came again, weaker now. "Help me..."

This is real. Jim's training had covered a lot of things. But not this. *Should I break in? Wait for the police?*

Twenty minutes felt like forever.

He couldn't just stand here.

Jim's eyes fell on a ceramic flowerpot beside the back steps, a small angel painted on its side. *What are the odds?* Lifting it, he found a key. He half-laughed. Hadn't he once mocked this kind of thing in a story?

Inside, he discovered Mrs. Wexley in her living room, pinned beneath a small bookcase. Books and knickknacks scattered around her like fallen leaves. Her face was pale, lips dry. Her right leg bent at an unnatural angle.

"Oh, honey," she whispered when she saw him. "I've been stuck here since yesterday morning."

Jim carefully moved the bookcase aside, then grabbed a pillow from the couch to support her head. In the kitchen, he found a glass and filled it with water, helping her sip slowly. He redialed 911, telling the dispatcher what he'd discovered and requesting an ambulance.

Twenty minutes later, paramedics were loading Mrs. Wexley onto a stretcher. She gripped Jim's hand as they wheeled her past.

"I prayed for an angel," she said. "And here you are."

After the ambulance disappeared down the dirt road, Jim sat in his truck for a long moment. His eyes drifted to the prayer card corner peeking from the visor. He pulled it out and read the prayer again:

"St. Gabriel, faithful messenger of God, you announced the coming of our Savior to the world. Help us to hear God's voice in our daily lives and to respond with willing hearts. Guide us to be messengers of His love and mercy to those in need."

Jim tucked the card back in place, started the engine, and continued his route.

For the first time since starting this job, he understood he was exactly where he was supposed to be. He wasn't crafting stories about heroes anymore. But he was still delivering something that mattered. One letter at a time.

OPENING PITCH

ather Joe yanked open the heavy hospital door, car keys already in hand. Seventeen parishioners visited. Seventeen prayers offered. The stomach bug tearing through the elderly had been merciless this week, but his flock had needed him.

"Father!" Mrs. Kowalski had called from her bed as the door began to close. "You tell those Tigers they got our prayers tonight."

Joe paused, grinning ear to ear. "They won't need luck, Mrs. K. They've got God on their side."

Her laughter followed him down the hall.

His phone buzzed. Keith again.

Dude, where are you? National anthem in 20 minutes. These seats are INSANE.

Joe thumbed back quickly: *On my way.*

Forty-one years old today. Same number of years since the Tigers won it all. Game One. World Series—tonight. Four rows behind third base, thanks to his brother's law-firm connections. He'd been dreaming about this since he was twelve. The parking-garage elevator couldn't come fast enough.

"Excuse me!"

A woman's voice, breathless. Joe turned.

Maybe fifty. Silver-streaked hair pulled tight. Faded jeans. Ripped sweatshirt. A face tanned by the sun.

"Are you a priest?"

Joe touched his collar. "Guilty as charged. A Catholic one, if that matters."

Then he noticed the wadded tissue in her hands. Tear stains on both cheeks. The quiver of her lower lip.

"You okay, miss?"

"My dad—" Her voice cracked. "He's dying. He asked for Last Rites, but our pastor is stuck in traffic on 75. The doctors say..." She swallowed hard. "They say maybe an hour."

Joe's keys suddenly felt heavy in his palm. His phone buzzed again. He didn't look.

"What's your dad's name?"

"Hank. Hank Morrison. We're Lutheran, but he's a believer, and I thought—" Her voice caught. Tears welled.

St. Joseph, help me be where I'm needed, Joe thought.

"Lead the way."

* * *

ROOM 312 SMELLED of antiseptic and something else. The approaching end. Hank Morrison lay propped against pillows, oxygen cannula in his nose, eyes closed. His breathing was shallow, labored.

Joe slipped his phone to silent and knelt beside the bed.

Hank's eyes opened—pale blue, clouded but aware.

"Hank? I'm Father Joe. Your daughter asked me to come."

The old man's gaze found his daughter, then returned to Joe. "You...Catholic?"

"Different churches," Joe said softly, taking Hank's hand. "Same God. We're all His children, loved from our first breath"—he squeezed gently—"to our last."

Hank's fingers tightened around his.

He made the sign of the cross over Hank. "Through this holy

anointing may the Lord in his love and mercy help you with the grace of the Holy Spirit."

Joe's voice grew stronger, carrying the ancient words: "May the Lord who frees you from sin save you and raise you up. Into your hands, Lord, I commend his spirit."

Hank's breathing seemed to ease as Joe continued the prayers for the dying, his thumb tracing a small cross on the old man's forehead.

"Go forth, Christian soul, from this world in the name of God the almighty Father who created you..."

When he finished, Hank's eyes were shut. As Joe stood, Hank's daughter collapsed into his arms, sobbing. She held on tight. He didn't let go.

"Thank you," she whispered against his shoulder. "Thank you."

Joe held her until her breathing steadied. When she finally pulled back, he placed a gentle hand on her shoulder. "He knew he was loved."

She nodded, wiping her eyes with the tissue. "Will you... would you mind staying just another minute? I don't want to be alone when..."

Joe glanced toward the door, then back at Hank's still form. The old man's breathing had grown even more shallow. "Of course."

They stood together in the quiet room, watching over Hank Morrison as his breath grew softer, slower, until it finally stopped altogether. Joe made the sign of the cross and whispered a final prayer.

"He's home," he said quietly.

Only then did Joe step into the hallway, his keys still clutched in his palm, wondering when he'd stopped thinking about baseball.

In the elevator, Joe finally checked his phone. Ten messages from Keith. The last one: *Game's starting. WHERE ARE YOU???*

The elevator dinged. Parking level 3.

Joe looked at the column of messages, then typed: *Exactly where God needed me to be. On my way.*

SONG OF HOPE

*L*ani's knee bounced as she sat in Dr. Hartwell's sterile office, watching him flip through her chart. The walls were covered with diplomas and throat anatomy posters that made her stomach clench. Ryan squeezed her hand from the chair beside her.

"I should have come to these appointments sooner," she'd told him that morning. "Should have insisted."

"You're here now," he'd said. "That's what matters."

But looking at Dr. Hartwell's expression, she wondered if "now" was too late.

"The tests confirm what we suspected," he said, finally looking up. "Spasmodic Dysphonia."

The words hit like cold water. She'd Googled it, of course, after the referral. Read the clinical descriptions, watched the YouTube videos of people whose voices sounded strangled, broken. Just like hers.

"But there are treatments, right?" She leaned forward, forcing the words out. "Botox injections? Speech therapy?"

Dr. Hartwell removed his glasses, cleaning them slowly. "Those can help manage symptoms. In some cases, patients see significant improvement."

"Some cases," Ryan repeated, the tone of her brother's voice mirroring her internal angst. "What about Lani's case specifically?"

The pause stretched too long. "Her condition is quite advanced. The muscle spasms are severe, and they're affecting multiple muscle groups in her larynx."

Lani gripped her thighs. "What does that mean for my career?" The question was barely audible.

"Ms. Torres, I think we need to focus on preserving what voice function you have for daily communication."

He met her stare.

No. Don't say it. Don't you dare—

"I'm sorry." Dr. Hartwell removed his glasses. "But a professional singing career... it's no longer realistic."

Her knee stopped bouncing. The room went silent except for the hum of fluorescent lights and the distant sound of traffic outside.

And just like that, everything she'd worked for since she was twelve years old. The voice lessons. The coffee-shop gigs. The years of rejection before that miraculous recording contract—all of it evaporated.

The ride home was torture. Ryan had offered to drive, but she'd refused, needing something to control. Now she sat at red lights listening to the radio, every note a reminder of what she'd lost. A song came on—one she'd written but that had been given to another artist when her voice started failing six months ago. The label called it "creative differences." She knew better.

Ryan was waiting when she pulled into her driveway, leaning against his truck with that protective look he'd worn since they were kids. After their parents died in the accident, he'd become her guardian at nineteen, sacrificing his college plans to raise her. He'd been at every school concert, every open-mic night, every recording session. Her biggest fan and fiercest protector.

"Don't take off your shoes," he said as she reached the front door.

She stared at him blankly.

"Father James is waiting for us at St. Bernadette's."

"Ryan, I can't—"

"You can. We can." He took her hand, the same way he used to when she'd wake up screaming from nightmares about the crash. "Please. Just trust me."

The church parking lot felt like foreign territory. She hadn't been inside since signing her recording contract two years ago. Success had been intoxicating. The late-night studio sessions, the industry parties, the validation of having her voice compared to Sara Bareilles. Faith had seemed like something for people who needed comfort, not for someone whose dreams were coming true.

How quickly things changed.

Inside, the familiar scent of incense and old wood wrapped around her like a memory. Father James stood at the altar holding two long candles, his face kind but serious.

"Lani." His voice carried the warmth she remembered from childhood. "I'm glad you came."

She wanted to tell him about the diagnosis, about the career that had just imploded, about how God seemed to have abandoned her just when she needed Him most. Instead, she just stood there, frozen.

Ryan nudged her forward across the polished tile. When she reached the altar, Father James crossed the candles, making an X. "This is the feast day of St. Blaise," he said softly. "He was a physician who understood that healing comes in many forms."

The candles felt cool against her throat as he placed them gently on either side of her neck. He prayed.

Lani waited for something—warmth, peace, the sensation of healing. Instead, she felt only the weight of ritual and the ache of disappointed hope.

The drive home was as quiet as the one from the doctor's office.

Two days passed in a haze of phone calls she couldn't bring herself to answer. Her manager, her label, her booking agent—all wanting to know about the "vocal rest" she'd been taking. Ryan brought her meals and tried to start conversations that died in the silence of her grief.

On the third day, she cried so hard that blood vessels broke around her eyes, leaving her looking like she'd been in a fight. Which, in a way, she had.

That night, Ryan knocked softly on her bedroom door before entering. He didn't say anything about her appearance, just set a pen and notepad on her nightstand and kissed her forehead.

"Sometimes," he said quietly, "the only way out is through."

Lani stared at the blank pages for hours after he left. Her throat felt raw from crying, her voice reduced to whispers and croaks. She picked up the pen three times and set it down again.

Finally, sometime after midnight, words began to flow:

> *When God takes your voice away*
> *Do you learn to listen?*
> *When dreams shatter like glass*
> *Do the pieces still glisten?*
>
> *I believe my life on shifting sand*
> *On notes that flew like birds*
> *Now Silence is my native land*
> *And broken are my words*

The words poured out. Every ounce of pain, rage, and shattered faith. Every memory of Ryan's quiet love, the prayers she'd heard him whispering through the walls when he thought she was asleep. Her anger at a God who gave gifts only to snatch them away. But also something else. A recognition that maybe she'd been singing for the wrong reasons, chasing the wrong kind of love, from the wrong kind of people.

When she finished, dawn was breaking through her bedroom curtains. She read the lyrics back slowly, her damaged voice barely a whisper. There was no question—this was her best song yet. Not because of its commercial potential, but because it came from a place deeper than technique or ambition. A place that reflected Him and His love, not her own desires.

Ryan appeared with breakfast and tea, setting the tray on her desk.

His eyes took in her tear-stained face, the pages covered in her handwriting, the faint melody she was still humming.

"You look... different," he said carefully.

She held up the notebook, offering a small smile. The first real one in days.

His smile was bigger as he read the lyrics. "This is beautiful, Lani. Really beautiful."

She hummed the melody for him, her voice cracking and wavering but carrying the song's heart. When she finished, she scribbled a note on the margin: *Tomorrow. I'll sing it. But not for me.*

"Tomorrow?" Ryan asked, reading over her shoulder. "You sure?"

"Not for record labels," she whispered, her voice barely audible but clear in its purpose. "Not for money or fame. For healing. To lead others to Him."

Ryan pulled her into a hug, and for the first time since the diagnosis, Lani felt something that might have been hope. Her voice was broken, but maybe that was exactly what the world needed to hear. That broken things could still make beautiful music, that God's love didn't depend on perfection, and that sometimes losing everything was the only way to find what really mattered.

Outside her window, the morning sun painted everything gold, and somewhere in her chest, a new song was already beginning.

THE LONG WAY HOME

*M*ikey traced the crack in Dad's watch band as he unlocked the church basement. Five-thirty a.m., same as every weekday for the past twenty years. *No.* He rubbed his eyes. *Twenty-one years.* Saint Bernadette's custodial job wasn't glamorous, but it paid the bills and came with something he'd forgotten he needed.

Quiet.

The old boiler rumbled to life with his touch. Trustworthy, like everything else built before he was born. Unlike the promises people made these days.

His phone buzzed. A text from Jimmy: *Still on for dinner Sunday? Maria's making her famous sauce.*

Mikey stared at the screen. Three months since that awkward phone call from his brother. A handful of lunches and two dinners that went better than expected. A sister-in-law who treated him like family instead of the brother who "never amounted to much."

He typed back: *Yeah. Looking forward to it.*

Not entirely true, but not a lie either.

The morning routine calmed him, helping clear his mind. He'd start in the nave, sweeping and dusting. Then, he'd polish the pews, replacing burnt-out votive candles. Father James emerged from the sacristy as Mikey finished mopping the sanctuary.

"Morning, Miguel."

"Morning, Father."

"The McKenna family asked me to thank you again. Said you did beautiful work on Mrs. McKenna's headstone."

Mikey shrugged. His weekend stone-cleaning business barely broke even, but something about restoring weathered memorials felt right. Like he was giving families back a piece of their history.

"Just soap and water, mostly."

Father James laid his hand on Mikey's shoulder. "Sometimes the simplest gifts matter most."

By noon, Mikey was replacing light bulbs in the fellowship hall when he heard shouting from the parking lot. Through the window, he saw a woman standing in front of a beat-up minivan, arguing with someone on her phone, two small kids clinging to her legs.

"I don't care what the landlord says!" Her voice carried through the glass. "I paid last month's rent! Please check your records... please."

The call ended with her throwing the phone into her purse, which fell from her hands onto the pavement. She stood there, shoulders sagging, while the kids—maybe four and six—stared up at her with that look that children get when they sense their world isn't safe.

Mikey recognized the expression. He'd worn it himself decades prior when Dad came back from Vietnam, when Mom started forgetting names, when Jimmy left for college, then the big city, and never really came back.

The woman noticed him watching and started toward the church entrance. He met her in the vestibule.

"I'm sorry," she said, voice shaky. "I know this isn't... I mean, we're not even Catholic. But I saw the cross and thought maybe..."

"What's your name?"

"Sarah. Sarah Chen. These are my boys, David and Luke."

The younger boy hid behind his mother's legs. The older one—David—studied Mikey with serious eyes.

"You guys hungry?" Mikey asked.

Sarah's chin trembled. "We haven't eaten since yesterday."

Mikey thought about his own lunch—leftover pizza and some homemade garlic bread from Sunday dinner at Jimmy's. Maria had sent him home with enough food for a week, like she always did.

"Follow me."

In the small custodial office, Mikey pulled a pair of containers from the mini-fridge. Pizza, garlic bread, even some of those fancy cookies Maria made from scratch. He heated everything in the microwave while Sarah explained.

Evicted that morning. Landlord claimed she'd missed rent, but she had receipts. Didn't matter. Worse, her husband was deployed overseas. Submariner. Six-month tour. No contact. No family nearby. Living in their car until she could figure something out.

"The shelter's full," she said, watching her boys devour the pizza. "They said maybe tomorrow, but..."

Mikey's fingers found Dad's watch. The leather band was softer now, worn smooth by time and Jimmy's grip during those awkward dinners. His brother had insisted on giving it back, said Dad would've wanted the son who stayed to have it.

In his mind, he saw St. Martin—his father's namesake and the patron saint who'd shared his cloak with a beggar on a cold winter day. The saint who understood that sometimes the simplest act of sharing could change everything.

"There's a motel on Route 1," Mikey said. "Nothing fancy, but it's clean, weekly rates."

"I can't afford—"

"How much you got?"

Sarah hesitated. "Forty-three dollars."

Mikey glanced at the cracked watch, heard again Father James's words: "The simplest gifts..." He saw the boys, thin wrists and wide eyes, like sheep without a shepherd.

He pulled out his wallet. Two twenties and a ten. His gas money for the week, plus what he'd saved for groceries. But the boys were still eating like they hadn't seen food in days, and Sarah's eyes held the same hollow look he'd seen in Mom's face those last months when the bills kept coming.

He handed her the fifty dollars.

"This is just to get you started. Father James knows people." He rubbed the back of his neck. "Social services, job placement. He'll help you figure out the rest."

"I can't take this."

"Yes, you can." Mikey's voice was gentle but firm. "Sometimes we all need someone to help us find our way home."

David looked up from his pizza. "Are you an angel?"

Mikey almost laughed. Him? An angel? If this kid only knew all the bad things he'd done. How many times he had to ask for forgiveness. From his parents. His ex-wife. God. "Nah, kid. Just a guy with a mop and a couple bucks to spare."

After they left—Sarah clutching Father James's card and Mikey's phone number—he finished his shift with empty pockets but something lighter in his chest.

That evening, he called Jimmy.

"Hey, brother."

"Mikey? Everything okay?"

"Yeah." Mikey smiled, watching the sunset through his apartment window. "Everything's good. Just wanted to hear your voice."

"Well, that's... nice. Maria's making extra sauce for Sunday. Said to tell you it freezes well."

"Tell her thanks. For everything."

A pause. "Mikey, you sure you're okay?"

"Just wanted to tell you that I'm glad we've reconnected." He touched the watch face, feeling the familiar crack in the crystal. "And that I love you."

A pause. Then Jimmy's voice, softer: "I love you too, Mikey."

The little boy's question echoed in his mind: *Are you an angel?* This time he chuckled. Probably not. Definitely not. But tonight, for the first time in years, he felt like he might be exactly who he was supposed to be.

St. Martin's kind of angel, maybe. The ordinary kind. The kind with calloused hands and just enough to share.

And maybe, in God's eyes, that was everything.

SAINT ISIDORE'S FIELD

*T*om Sullivan stared at the certified the words swimming before his eyes. *Final Notice. Foreclosure proceedings will commence October 15th unless payment in full is received.*

Three weeks. One hundred and five years of Sullivan family farming, and he had three weeks.

He crumpled the letter and hurled it toward the barn, watching it bounce off the faded red siding and land in the dirt where his grandfather had first taught him to milk cows. Where his father had shown him how to read the sky for weather. Where he'd planned to teach his own son, before Jake decided that college and the city held more promise than corn and soybeans.

The September sun beat down mercilessly, the same sun that had baked his fields to dust for three straight months. Insurance covered acts of God, his agent had explained, but apparently God's silence didn't qualify.

Tom climbed into the cab of his rusted John Deere and surveyed the corn that remained. Forty acres of stunted stalks, maybe enough to keep the lights on another month if he could harvest it himself. But harvest season waited for no man, and one person couldn't work fast enough to beat the weather. Or Father Time.

His phone buzzed. A text from his neighbor Pete: *Hiring crew from town. $10/hour. Need help finding workers?*

Tom deleted the message. Ten dollars an hour he didn't have for work he'd done by himself for thirty years. His father would have called it pride. Tom called it arithmetic.

The dust cloud appeared on County Road 18 around noon, growing larger until it became a battered pickup truck with Mexican plates and a camper shell. Tom's jaw tightened. Every year they came through, following the harvest north, taking jobs from locals who needed the work. And every year he told them no. *Hell no.*

The truck pulled into his driveway and stopped. A man about Tom's age climbed out—stocky, weathered, wearing work clothes that had seen better years. A woman emerged from the passenger side, followed by two teenagers and a boy who couldn't have been more than ten.

"Señor," the man called out, approaching with his hat in his hands. "My name is Marvin Lopez. We are looking for work. Harvest work."

"Can't help you," Tom said without getting down from the tractor. "Not hiring."

Marvin gestured toward the corn. "Looks ready." His eyes swept from the field toward the house and barn, before settling on Tom again. "One man, very hard to finish in time."

"I'll manage."

"Sí, claro." Marvin replaced his hat. "But if you change your mind, we work for food and place to sleep. Nothing more."

Tom stared at him. "You're telling me you'll harvest forty acres for three meals a day?"

The woman stepped forward, touching Marvin's arm gently. She spoke in rapid Spanish, her voice urgent.

"My wife says the girl—" Marvin gestured to the youngest child. "She has not eaten since yesterday. We spent last money on gas to get here."

Tom felt something twist in his chest. The girl stood beside the truck, thin shoulders hunched, staring at the ground with that hollow look Tom recognized from his own mirror some mornings.

"There's a McDonald's in town," Tom said finally. He dug his hand into his pocket, fishing out a crumpled twenty-dollar bill. *What am I doing?* Then, without answering his own question, he hopped from his tractor and handed the money to Marvin. "It's about ten miles south."

Marvin tipped his hat as he palmed the gift. "Sí, muchos gracias, Señor." He herded his family back toward the truck.

As they drove away, Tom sat—calculating. Forty acres. Two weeks if he was lucky. Maybe three if the weather held. Working sixteen-hour days, he might—might—get half of it in before the rains came.

That evening, Tom sat on his porch with a beer and a bologna sandwich, listening to the corn rustling in the breeze. Somewhere out there, Marvin's family was probably bedding down in their truck, the kids wondering when they'd eat again.

He thought about his grandfather's stories of the Depression, when neighbors helped neighbors because survival wasn't a solo sport. When his grandmother would cook extra and leave plates on the porch for whoever needed them.

Different times, his father used to say. *People were better then.*

Maybe. Or maybe they were just more honest about needing each other.

Tom finished his beer and went into the cellar, where he kept sleeping bags for the occasional hunting trip with Jake. Four of them, dusty but serviceable. In the kitchen, he opened cabinets and started pulling out canned goods, rice, and beans. Enough for several days.

He loaded everything into his pickup and drove toward town, scanning the roadside for a battered truck with Mexican plates.

He found them parked behind the abandoned gas station on the outskirts of town, huddled around a small camp stove. Marvin looked up as Tom's headlights swept over them.

"Señor?"

Tom climbed out, arms full of sleeping bags. "Offer still stand? Work for food and a place to sleep?"

Marvin's face broke into a slow smile. "Sí, señor. It stands."

"Tom," he said, extending his hand. "Name's Tom Sullivan."

"Marvin Lopez." The handshake was firm, calloused. "This is my family. Isabella, my wife. My sons Carlos and Miguel. And this is Lucia."

Tom offered each child a warm smile. "You can set up camp in the barn," he said, turning back to Marvin. "There's electricity, running water, a bathroom. We'll start at sunrise."

As the family gathered their belongings, Tom heard Marvin speaking quietly to his wife in Spanish. She looked toward Tom and smiled, pressing her hands together in a gesture that needed no translation.

"Gracias," she said. "Dios te bendiga."

God bless you. Tom couldn't remember the last time anyone had said that to him and meant it.

The next morning, Tom found Marvin already in the field at dawn, on his knees beside the first row of corn, head bowed. Praying, Tom realized. The man was praying over someone else's crop.

Marvin looked up as Tom approached. "In Mexico, we always ask God and San Isidro to bless the harvest. Saint Isidore, you say in English. He understands farmers."

Tom nodded, not sure what to say. He'd stopped asking God for much of anything years ago.

"San Isidro was a farmer too," Marvin continued, standing and brushing dirt from his knees. "Worked another man's land his whole life. But the angels helped him plow when he stopped to pray."

"Angels?"

Marvin smiled. "Sí. When the other workers complained that Isidore spent too much time praying, the boss went to check. Found Isidore praying in the field while angels finished the plowing."

Tom glanced at the endless rows of corn. "Could use some of those angels right about now."

They worked in silence for the first hour, Tom showing Marvin the rhythm of the harvest—when to cut, how to load the wagons, where to store the ears. But Marvin's hands seemed to know the work already, moving with the confidence of someone born to farming.

Carlos and Miguel, the teenagers, worked alongside their father with quiet efficiency. Their mother prepared lunch in the barn while Lucia followed the adults, carrying water and asking endless questions about American farming, albeit in broken English.

By noon, they'd covered more ground than Tom had managed in three days of working alone.

"How long you been farming?" Tom asked as they shared lunch in the shade of the barn.

"All my life," Marvin said. "My father, his father. We had small farm, ten acres. Corn, beans, peppers. Good life until the drought."

"I'm sorry."

"Is not your fault, Mr. Tom. Is life. But we know how to work. Is all we know."

That afternoon, as Tom watched Marvin's family move through his field, he found himself thinking about Saint Isidore. A man who'd worked someone else's land his whole life and somehow found holiness in it.

Maybe that was the secret. Not owning the land, but serving it.

By the end of the third day, they'd harvested twenty-five acres. Tom had never seen corn picked so efficiently, so carefully. Nothing wasted, nothing rushed. Marvin and his boys treated each stalk like it mattered.

"Mi abuelo taught me that work is prayer," Marvin said, "when you do it with love. Every plant is gift from God. We take only what we need, waste nothing."

Tom thought about his own grandfather's lessons, how they'd been about efficiency and profit margins. Marvin's grandfather had taught something different.

That night, a storm rolled in. Tom woke to thunder and the sound of rain drumming on his roof. His first thought was relief—they'd beaten the weather. His second was worry about the family in the barn.

He pulled on boots and a raincoat and ran across the yard. Inside the barn, he found the Lopez family gathered around their small camp stove, speaking in low voices. Isabella was bandaging Carlos's hand with strips torn from a towel.

"What happened?"

"Cut himself on the equipment," Marvin said. "Nothing serious."

Tom looked at the makeshift bandage, the family's meager supplies scattered around their sleeping area. "Come to the house. I've got a first-aid kit."

"No, no," Isabella protested. "We fine here."

"Isabella," Tom said gently. "It's pouring rain and your son is hurt. Come to the house. Por favor."

In his kitchen, Tom cleaned and properly bandaged the boy's cut while Isabella fretted in Spanish. Marvin translated apologetically.

"She says thank you, but she is sorry to be trouble."

"Tell her you're not trouble. Tell her—" Tom paused, looking around his empty house. "Tell her it's been a long time since this place felt like a home."

When Marvin translated, Tom saw Isabella's eyes filled with tears. She spoke rapidly, gesturing toward Tom.

"She says you are like San Isidro. He shared everything, even when he had little."

"I'm not a saint," Tom said. "Just a farmer who's about to lose his farm."

"Maybe is same thing," Marvin said quietly.

The next morning dawned clear. Two more days of harvest, and they'd have the entire crop in. Tom found himself moving slower, finding reasons to extend the work. When this was over, Marvin's family would move on to the next farm, the next town. And Tom would be alone again, waiting for the bank to take what was left.

On the final day, as they loaded the last wagon, Marvin found Tom sitting on his tractor, staring at the empty field.

"You did it, Mr. Tom. All forty acres."

"We did it," Tom corrected. "Couldn't have managed without you."

Marvin was quiet for a moment. "What will you do now?"

Tom pulled out the bank letter, now soft from folding and refolding. "Sell the crop, pay what I can. Maybe delay things a few more months."

"And then?"

"Don't know. Never done anything but farm."

Marvin nodded toward his family, who were packing their belongings into the truck. "We understand. Is hard to start over."

That evening, as the Lopez family prepared to leave, Tom found himself calculating numbers in his head. The harvest would bring maybe twelve thousand dollars. Enough to delay foreclosure but not prevent it. He'd still lose the farm, just later.

But what if...

"Marvin," he called out as the family gathered around their truck. "What if you didn't leave?"

"Señor?"

Tom took a deep breath. "I've been thinking about Saint Isidore. You said he worked someone else's land his whole life."

"Sí."

"What if that's not failure? What if that's partnership?"

Marvin frowned. "No comprendo, Mr. Tom."

"The bank wants this farm," Tom said. "They'll get it eventually. But what if, instead of losing it to them, I found a way to share it?" He took a deep breath. "Listen—you know farming. Your family knows farming. Maybe… maybe together we could make it work."

"Mr. Tom," Marvin said slowly. "We have no money. No papers—"

"I don't care about papers. I care about people who know how to pray over corn and treat every plant like it matters." Tom looked at the field they'd harvested together. "My grandfather always said that land belongs to whoever loves it most. I think that might be you."

Isabella spoke rapidly to Marvin, her voice excited. He translated. "She asks if you are serious."

"Dead serious. We split everything. Profits, losses, decisions. Equal partners."

Marvin was quiet for a long moment, looking at his sons, who were listening intently despite the language barrier. He glanced at the field, then at his wife, who was nodding encouragingly.

"San Isidro," Marvin said finally, "he never owned land. But God blessed his work anyway."

"So?"

Marvin stuck out his hand and smiled. "So maybe angels come in different forms than we expect."

Tom returned the smile as their hands met. "Sometimes they come as a family with nothing but calloused hands and the wisdom to know that land, like love, was meant to be shared."

THE SAINTS AMONG US

A BRIEF GUIDE

Saint Rita of Cascia (May 22)
Patron Saint of Impossible Cases and Difficult Marriages

Rita Lotti was forced into an arranged marriage with a violent, unfaithful man in 15th-century Italy. For eighteen years, she endured abuse while praying for her husband's conversion. Her patience and forgiveness eventually softened his heart, though he was murdered shortly after his spiritual transformation. Rita then faced the challenge of preventing her sons from seeking revenge.

After her husband's death and her sons' eventual deaths from illness, Rita joined an Augustinian convent. She spent her final years in prayer and service, bearing the stigmata—a crown of thorns that appeared on her forehead. She became known for interceding in hopeless situations, especially troubled marriages.

"Holy Rita, you who endured so much pain in your marriage, intercede for us who struggle to hold love together when it's falling apart.

* * *

Saint John Bosco (January 31)

Patron Saint of Youth and Students

Born into poverty in 19th-century Italy, Giovanni Bosco dedicated his life to educating and caring for street children. Known as "Don Bosco," he believed that young people needed reason, religion, and kindness rather than punishment to flourish. He founded the Salesian order and established schools, workshops, and churches throughout Italy.

Don Bosco's approach was revolutionary for his time. He treated difficult youth with respect and saw potential in every child. His famous quote captures his philosophy: "It is not enough to love young people; they must know they are loved." He died in 1888 and was canonized in 1934.

"It is not enough to love young people; they must know they are loved."

* * *

Saint Dymphna (May 15)
Patron Saint of Mental Illness, Abuse Survivors, and Runaways

Born to Irish royalty in the seventh century, Dymphna fled her homeland when her father, driven by grief and mental illness after her mother's death, sought to force her into an inappropriate relationship. Accompanied by her confessor, St. Gerebernus, she escaped to Belgium, seeking safety and sanctuary far from home.

In Geel, Belgium, Dymphna devoted herself to caring for the mentally ill and those suffering from emotional trauma—people who society had abandoned. Her father eventually tracked her down and, when she refused to return, killed both her and her confessor. The townspeople, moved by her martyrdom and healing work, continued her mission of compassionate care.

Geel became renowned throughout Europe for its humane treatment of mental illness, with its families taking in patients as their own. Dymphna's legacy reminds us that healing requires both sanctuary and community, and that sometimes the bravest thing we can do is seek help when we need it most.

"St. Dymphna, comfort those who struggle with mental illness and trauma. Help us create safe places for healing and grant courage to those who must flee to find safety."

* * *

Saint Thérèse of Lisieux (October 1)
Patron Saint of Missionaries and "The Little Flower"

Born Marie-Françoise-Thérèse Martin in 1873, Thérèse entered the Carmelite convent at age fifteen and died of tuberculosis just nine years later. Despite her brief life, she became one of the most beloved saints through her revolutionary approach to holiness, which she called "the little way."

Thérèse believed that God is reached not through extraordinary deeds but through small acts done with extraordinary love. Rather than attempting grand gestures, she found holiness in daily kindnesses: smiling at difficult people, helping with simple tasks, offering small sacrifices with joy. Her approach made sainthood accessible to ordinary people living ordinary lives.

She promised to "spend my heaven doing good on earth" and to shower roses of grace from above. Her feast day reminds us that the path to holiness is open to everyone, regardless of circumstances, and that God values the love behind our smallest actions as much as great martyrdoms.

"Do little things with great love. I will spend my heaven doing good on earth."

* * *

Saint Christopher (July 25)
Patron Saint of Travelers

Though his historical existence is debated, Christopher's legend speaks to the desire to serve Christ in practical ways. According to tradition, he was a giant who sought to serve the most powerful king. After converting to Christianity, he used his great strength to carry travelers across a dangerous river.

One day, a small child asked for passage. As Christopher carried him, the child became impossibly heavy. The child revealed himself as Christ, saying Christopher had carried the weight of the world's sins. "Christopher" means "Christ-bearer," and his medal remains popular among travelers seeking protection.

"St. Christopher, protect us as we journey through life, and help us carry Christ to others."

* * *

Saint Gabriel the Archangel (September 29)

Patron Saint of Messengers, Postal Workers, and Communications

One of three archangels named in Scripture, Gabriel serves as God's chief messenger, announcing the most important events in salvation history. His name means "God is my strength," and he appears at pivotal moments: announcing John the Baptist's birth to Zechariah and, most famously, delivering the Annunciation to Mary that she would bear the Son of God.

Gabriel's messages often came to people facing impossible circumstances—an elderly, barren couple and a young virgin. In our modern world, he has become patron of all who carry messages, from postal workers to anyone who helps connect people across distances. The archangel reminds us that every message we deliver can be a vehicle for God's grace.

"St. Gabriel, faithful messenger of God, help us to hear God's voice in our daily lives and to respond with willing hearts. Guide us to be messengers of His love and mercy to those in need."

* * *

Saint Joseph (March 19)

Patron Saint of Fathers, Workers, and the Universal Church

The foster father of Jesus and husband of Mary, Joseph was a carpenter who embodied quiet strength and faithful obedience. When faced with Mary's unexpected pregnancy, he chose trust over doubt, accepting God's plan despite not understanding it fully. Scripture tells us little about Joseph's words—only his actions—making him a model of humble service and protective love.

Joseph died before Jesus began his public ministry, yet his influence shaped the Son of God's earthly life. He taught Jesus his trade, provided for the Holy Family, and protected them during their flight to Egypt. His feast day reminds us that holiness often looks like ordinary work done with extraordinary love.

"St. Joseph, help me be where I'm needed."

* * *

Saint Blaise (February 3)

Patron Saint of Throat Ailments

A physician who became a bishop in fourth-century Armenia, Blaise was known for his healing ministry during the persecution of Christians under Emperor Diocletian. Legend tells of him healing both humans and animals, including saving a child who was choking on a fishbone—which led to his patronage of those with throat ailments.

When persecution intensified, Blaise retreated to a cave where wild animals would come to him for healing. He was eventually captured and martyred around 316 AD. The blessing of throats with crossed candles on his feast day continues this healing tradition, reminding us that God's grace can work through physical means.

"Through the intercession of St. Blaise, bishop and martyr, may God deliver you from every disease of the throat and from every other illness."

* * *

Saint Martin of Tours (November 11)

Patron Saint of Soldiers, Beggars, and France

A Roman soldier who became a bishop, Martin embodied Christian charity before his full conversion. The defining moment of his life occurred on a bitter winter day in Amiens when he encountered a nearly naked beggar at the city gates. Without hesitation, Martin drew his sword, cut his military cloak in half, and gave one piece to the beggar.

That night, Martin dreamed of Christ wearing the half-cloak, saying to the angels, "Martin, who is not yet baptized, clothed me with this robe." Martin was baptized soon after and eventually became Bishop of Tours, serving the poor and founding monasteries until his death in 397 AD.

Martin's spontaneous act of sharing what little he had reminds us that the most profound acts of charity often require no planning, only a heart ready to respond to immediate need.

"Lord, help me see Christ in those who have less than I do, and give me the courage to share what I have."

* * *

Saint Isidore the Farmer (May 15)

Patron Saint of Farmers, Rural Communities, and Madrid

Born around 1070 to a poor family in Madrid, Isidore worked as a farmhand his entire life on the estate of Juan de Vargas. Though he never owned land, he treated every acre as sacred ground, beginning each day with Mass before heading to the fields. His fellow workers often complained that his devotion to prayer made him lazy, but their employer discovered something remarkable when he went to investigate.

According to legend, while Isidore knelt in prayer at the edge of the field, angels continued his plowing with a team of white oxen. His crops consistently flourished, and he shared his modest harvest generously with those in need, trusting that God would provide. Isidore and his wife Maria lived simply, opening their home to travelers and feeding the hungry even when their own cupboard was nearly bare.

Isidore died in 1130 and was canonized in 1622 alongside Teresa of Avila, Ignatius of Loyola, and Francis Xavier. His feast day reminds us that honest work offered to God becomes prayer, and that the earth itself is a gift to be tended with reverence and shared with compassion.

"San Isidro, help us see all work as prayer and teach us to share the fruits of our labor with those in need."

AFTERWORD

In the past, if you'd asked me if I wanted to be a saint, I would have said sainthood was reserved for those who perform grand gestures—miracles, even—people with a connection to the holy that seemed unattainable for ordinary, broken people like me.

I couldn't have been more wrong.

Sainthood isn't about earthly validation or even titles. It's about offering help to those who need it and accepting help when it's offered to us. It's about loving not only when it feels right and good, but especially when it seems impossible or undeserved. It's about showing up. It's about saying yes to grace, one small choice at a time, until love becomes our native language.

The saints in these stories didn't set out to change the world. They just decided to love the person in front of them. Kim lighting a candle for an impossible marriage. Sam picking up The Odyssey. Father Joe missing the game to stay with a dying man. Ordinary people doing ordinary things with extraordinary love.

Maybe that's the most profound truth about sainthood: we're all called to it. The question isn't whether we're worthy—none of us are. The question is whether we're willing.

Hopefully, you found something of yourself in these stories. I know I did.

—C.E. Albanese

ABOUT THE AUTHOR

C.E. Albanese is an award-winning author and former U.S. Secret Service special agent. Winner of the 2021 Clive Cussler Adventure Writers Competition Grandmaster Award, his fiction has appeared in magazines and anthologies. He co-hosts *The Crew Reviews* podcast, interviewing renowned authors. His work spans multiple genres, drawing from his faith and law enforcement background to explore authentic human experiences.

Learn more at: www.cealbanese.com

ALSO BY C.E. ALBANESE